THIS BOOK BELONGS TO

Mango Allsorts
Brave and helpful; a very good friend indeed.

Bambang
Completely NOT-a-pig; new to the busy city.

Mango's papa

Mostly in his study; welcomes visitors from overseas.

VERY busy— please do not disturb!

Dr Cynthia Prickle-Posset

A neighbour with a net; doesn't like cake or children.

George-from-the-tree-in-the-park

Keeper of toffees; avoider of baths.

*For my "papa" Tom; who was good at puddings and
stories and kindness and who would have been happy
to share pancakes with a tapir.* P. F.

For Hilary, with love. C. V.

First published 2015 by Walker Books Ltd
87 Vauxhall Walk, London SE11 5HJ

This edition published 2016

2 4 6 8 10 9 7 5 3 1

Text © 2015 Polly Faber
Illustrations © 2015 Clara Vulliamy

The right of Polly Faber and Clara Vulliamy to be identified as author and illustrator
respectively of this work has been asserted by them in accordance with the Copyright,
Designs and Patents Act 1988

This book has been typeset in Veronan

Printed and bound in China

British Library Cataloguing in Publication Data:
a catalogue record for this book is available from the British Library

ISBN 978-1-4063-6714-0

www.walker.co.uk

Mango & BAMBANG

The Not-a-Pig

POLLY FABER
CLARA VULLIAMY

WALKER
BOOKS

Contents

Mango and the Muddle
8-43

Bambang's Pool
44-77

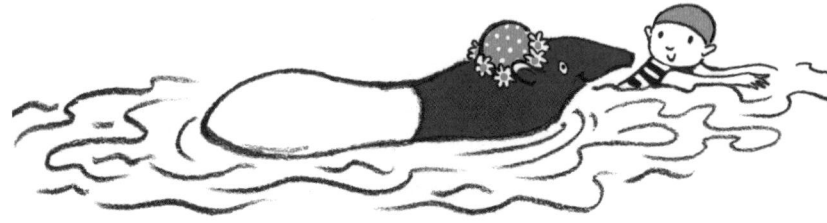

Bambang Puts On a Hat

78-111

The Song
of the Tapir
112-143

Mango and the Muddle

Mango Allsorts was a girl good at all sorts of things. That was not the same as being a good girl, but she was that, too. Most of the time.

She lived at the very top of a tall building in the middle of a very, VERY busy city.

She lived with her papa, who was also tall and very busy. He spent every day shut up in his study, trying to make books balance. This often took a long time. When, even *after* a long time, the books still wouldn't be balanced, Mango's papa got rather tired. On those days she made him her special buttered noodles.

That was one of the things Mango was good at.

She had a nearly black belt in karate, could jump off the highest board at the swimming pool without holding her nose, use the Sicilian Defence when playing chess and

wiggle her ears while sucking a lollipop.

She was also learning to play the clarinet. Sometimes the sounds that came out of the bottom were not exactly the sounds Mango had meant when she blew into the top,

but Mango
knew that she
just needed to keep
practising and soon
she would be good at
that, too.

Mango had a lot of time for
practising; her papa's long hours
balancing meant she had to find her
own things to do. Becoming good at
those things kept her busy. And being
busy was important, living in a very
busy city, full of other busy people being
good at things.

Because otherwise Mango might
have been a little lonely.

It was on a Wednesday that everything changed. It's important to note that it was a Wednesday. A Wednesday can seem a bit of a humpish, nothingish sort of day, but even humpish sorts of days can hold the unexpected.

In this case the unexpected WAS a hump.

Mango was on her way back from her karate lesson, thinking about how to make her side-thrust kick more effective, when she came to a zebra crossing. She was used to having to wait on the edge of the kerb for all the traffic to stop.

In the very busy city,

drivers were always in a rush and it

sometimes took them a while to notice

a girl wanting to cross.

But today the traffic was already stopped. In fact it was VERY stopped. Cars were jammed bumper to bumper up either side of the road, horns were being honked and some people had even got out of their vehicles and were shouting words they shouldn't have been shouting. It was all a bit of a muddle.

Sorting out a muddle was another thing Mango was good at.

In the middle of the crossing a small crowd had gathered round an obstruction. Mango couldn't see exactly what the obstruction was, but with a bit of wriggling and a few polite *Excuse me, please*s, she managed to squeeze through the forest of legs and find out.

You'll know that a zebra crossing is normally a perfectly flat affair of thick painted white lines. But on this particular Wednesday a small hill had sprouted unexpectedly in the middle. Two black stripes and one white one had risen out of the ground to create an obstacle the cars couldn't get past.

The small crowd were all arguing about where the hill had come from and what should be done about it.

"This is a disgrace! I shall be late for my hair appointment," said a stout man, who didn't seem to have any hair at all.

"It's the underground pipework gone wrong! I've always said the sewers in this city are not fit for purpose. Someone should inform the authorities," said a lady in an alarming hat.

"I say we dynamite it! Blow it up, I say. **Kaboom**, I say!" said an overexcited man, who kept poking the hump with his umbrella.

Mango noticed the hump was quivering. She knelt down and put a gentle hand on it. It was warm and a little bit hairy. She gave it a comforting scratch and then whispered, "Hello, my name is Mango. Please don't worry. Can I help you?"

Out of one of the black stripes a small, sad eye opened, peered at Mango, then blinked away a tear. The hump shifted a little and a long black snout unfurled. It sniffled against Mango's open palm in a damp, whiskery sort of way. Very, very softly, so softly in fact that nobody but Mango could hear it, the hump whispered the single warning:

Tiger!

Then the eye shut, the snout tucked in and the hump curled into a tight mound once more.

The quivering turned into violent shaking.

"*Eek!* It's alive! It's got NOSTRILS! It's a mutant sewer-pig! They're surging up from the pipes! They'll come out of our toilets and eat us in our beds at night!" shrieked the alarming hat lady.

"I read about mutant pigs in the paper, I'm sure of it," said the bald man, nodding in a definite sort of way. "Shocking."

"Send in the air force! Mobilize the army! Press the big red button that fires the big fat bomb!" The overexcited man was jumping from foot to foot and jabbing his umbrella in the air.

Mango made herself tall and folded her arms. She looked at them all. She spoke in her best voice-for-calming-people-who-are-being-silly. She was good at that, too.

"You are all being ridiculous. This is **NOT a pig**, or a danger. Anyone sensible can see this is clearly a **tapir** from the jungles of Malaysia. He must have taken a wrong turning somewhere along the way. I expect one tree looks much like another if you wander too far."

"A tapir? Never heard of it. Don't believe in it," said the bald man. Mango gave him a pitying look. The crowd began to go back to their vehicles. She knelt down and talked to the tapir once more.

"A tiger sounds very alarming. But I promise there isn't one now. Won't you uncurl and cross the road with me? I'm going home to make banana pancakes for my papa. We'd love you to join us."

Slowly, under Mango's encouraging strokes, the shaking first settled, then stopped ... and the hump changed shape. From out of the zebra crossing the black-and-white lines resolved themselves into a really rather marvellous black-and-white creature.

Have you ever met a tapir? You need to keep a careful watch for them when out and about; they are nervous animals, inclined to jumpiness and tend to hide when scared. It takes a very special person to be trusted by a tapir.

"Banana pancakes?" said the tapir, in a hopeful whisper. He didn't seem quite ready to move. "With syrup and cream, too, if you like," said Mango, gently. She sensed this was a tapir who should not be hurried.

HONK HONK!

BEEP BEEP!

The people in the traffic jam were less patient. A lot of rather noisy engine revving was beginning to happen. There were shouts of "Oh, come ON!" and "Move it along now!" too.

"I've never had syrup or cream OR a pancake before," said the tapir, his voice getting less whispery. "But I do like bananas very much indeed."

"Papa and I would be delighted to introduce you to all those things and more," said Mango. "Were you planning a long visit to the city? We have plenty of room for you to stay. I'm so sorry – I don't know your name." She glanced at the ever-growing traffic jam.

TING-A-LING-A-LING!

The overexcited man was now talking overexcitedly to a policeman on a motorbike, who was writing in a notebook. A line of cycle-rickshaws had joined the queue and their bells were ringing impatiently. So was the louder bell of the halted Express City Tram.

"My name is Bambang," said the tapir. "And your offer sounds very kind. I *am* a little tired. I ran a great distance and swam and there was a boat, I think, although I am not perfectly sure, but certainly more running. And there was a tiger ... a hungry tiger, you see..." As he spoke the tapir started to look anxious again, as if he might curl straight back into a ball.

Mango, conscious of a helicopter now starting to circle overhead, was quick to reassure him. "There are no tigers in the city, Bambang. Apart from in the zoo, perhaps, but they're safely locked up and kept very well fed, I should think."

Suddenly the policeman bellowed
through a megaphone:

ALL GIRLS AND POSSIBLE
MUTANT PIGS MUST
CLEAR THE THOROUGHFARE!

REPEAT – THOROUGHFARE
MUST BE CLEARED OF ALL PIGS
IMMEDIATELY, OR FORCIBLE
REMOVAL WILL BE EFFECTED.

He started to direct the cars
to one side, apparently making space
for something else to come through.

"No tigers at all?" The tapir peered up at Mango.

"None."

"Then I would very much like to try a pancake and maybe stay a *little* while. If you're sure it would be no trouble?" And with that, to Mango's relief, Bambang started to cross the road.

Her relief was short-lived.

They hadn't moved more than a couple of steps before there was an unfortunate setback.

The drivers, seeing the tapir start to move, all put their feet on their car pedals at once, creating a sudden, definitely TIGER-ish roar. This was enough to startle Bambang.

At the same time, he spotted something on the other side of the road that sent him curling up tight again.

"TIGER!" he shouted. The zebra crossing, or tapir not-crossing as it might more accurately have been called (zebra stripes being thin and zigzaggy and quite different, after all), was blocked once more.

Mango felt alarmed. She could see the policeman had been clearing cars to make way for a giant, scooping digger. That giant, scooping digger was now manoeuvring into position and lowering its giant scoop. There seemed little doubt that what it was intending to scoop was Bambang.

She looked across the road. She remembered that tapirs are known to have rather poor eyesight. She suddenly saw what had frightened Bambang.

"Well, this is quite a muddle," Mango said to herself.

She went up to the policeman. "Could I possibly borrow your megaphone for a moment?" she asked.

She stood firmly in front of the digger with her hand out. It juddered to a surprised stop.

Mango climbed on top of its scoop and addressed the waiting traffic.

THERE IS A TAPIR HERE. HE WILL CROSS THE ROAD BUT HE IS FEELING A BIT NERVOUS. HE HAS NEVER BEEN IN A BUSY CITY BEFORE, YOU SEE. I THINK IT WOULD BE VERY HELPFUL IF YOU COULD ALL TURN OFF YOUR ENGINES FOR A MOMENT AND STOP SHOUTING AND BEEPING AND RINGING YOUR BELLS AND THEN I CAN TALK TO HIM CALMLY AND WE WILL BE ON OUR WAY FOR BANANA PANCAKES VERY SHORTLY.

Mango started to hand back the megaphone, but then she put it to her lips again. "THANK YOU," she added.

There was a pause and then, one by one, the shouting people, the cars, the rickshaws, the tram and the digger fell silent. The helicopter moved discreetly away.

Mango leant down to the Bambang-shaped hump and talked soothingly into where she hoped his ear might be.

"Bambang, dear Bambang, there really, truly, honestly is no tiger. Did you perhaps see that tabby cat on the wall over there and *think* it was a tiger? I can see it might be very easy to confuse a close-up cat with a far-away tiger. If you'll only uncurl I can show you the difference. And then you can come home and meet Papa and eat bananas and try pancakes and stay." She tickled his white stripe.

Inside his ball, Bambang thought and thought some more. On the one foot there was the possibility of a tiger, on another was the promise of pancakes and on a third there was Mango. He had always been very keen on mangos. He didn't even need to use his fourth foot. He brought his head out again and crossed bravely to the pavement.

Walking home with her new friend, Mango found herself feeling not perfectly certain what having a tapir come to stay might involve.

And that was a very exciting feeling indeed.

Bambang's Pool

Bambang wriggled and pushed his snout through the small gap at the bottom of the window. The rain pitter-pattered against his nose. By stretching out his tongue as far as it would go, he could catch the drops as they fell. He gave a little sigh.

He'd been in the city a month.
A month full of sights undreamed of
when he'd run and run and swum and
hidden and run-some-more away from
the jungle. Bambang still hid, sometimes
several times a day, from possible tigers,
but he'd not met a single REAL one in all
that time. Instead he had met automatic
doors and ice cream and trams and
bubbles in fizzy lemonade and kites and
ticket turnstiles and so many
other wonderful things.
Best of all, he'd
met them all
with wonderful
Mango.

There was only one thing he missed.

Mango looked up from her chess board at the sigh. She had been trying out a new pawn opening.

"Oh, Bambang! What's the matter? Are you missing your pond?"

It couldn't be hidden. Tapirs love water. In his patch of jungle Bambang had lived near a cool pool of weed and mud where he'd wallowed and rolled his cares away. On days like this, when the rain came down, the smell brought back memories. It was all that he missed, but he DID miss it.

"Do you want me to run you a bath again?" asked Mango.

Bambang shook his head. He'd tried the bath, but it wasn't the same. The problem was not all of him fitted in it in one go. Either he had to drape his front legs over the edge, or hang his bottom out the back. It was undignified.

"I know!" said Mango, getting up from her chess board. "We'll go swimming. Properly. At the swimming baths."

Bambang's ears and snout both pricked up at that suggestion. He liked the idea.

What are your nearest swimming baths like? Do they have exciting things like wave machines and curly slides and bubbly bits? Or are they just a plain rectangle?

The very busy city where Mango lived had the rectangle sort. The very busy people didn't have time for curly slides.

There were two rectangles there. A small, deep one, with boards beside it for practising jumping and diving, and a long, thin one, divided into lanes for going up and down. Bambang looked at the diving boards with a keen interest. There were nothing like *them* in the jungle. He wanted to try one straight away.

Mango said it might be better to *start* with the up-and-down pool.

It was divided into three lanes, marked with firm notices that read SLOW, MEDIUM and FAST. Bambang and Mango looked at each other, not sure which one they should choose. The other people in the pool were no help.

In the **FAST** lane a man with a serious moustache was flapping his arms and kicking his legs in an energetic manner, but not moving anywhere at all.

The **SLOW** lane had a line of very old ladies, all bobbing and gliding like clockwork through the water.

It seemed rather full.

They settled for **MEDIUM.**

Bambang was just about to get in when a fierce man in a vest and shorts blew his whistle and pointed.

"The pig needs a hat: no hat, no swim," he said.

Mango rolled her eyes. "I'm so sorry, Bambang. A **pig** indeed! Come out of your ball; the lifeguard's NOT a tiger – just a big silly. You can borrow my spare swimming hat."

When he'd unrolled himself,
Bambang thought he'd never seen
anything as magnificent as Mango's
spare swimming hat. It was his first hat.
He liked it very much indeed.

They got in the water and began
to swim.

To start with Bambang was happy.
It was lovely to have the whole of
his body in the water
once more,

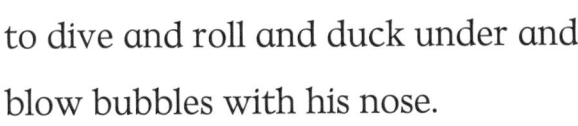

to dive and roll and duck under and
blow bubbles with his nose.

But it wasn't like his jungle pool.
The water smelt wrong and there was
no sticky mud to squish his toes into or
weed to play hide-and-seek with the
fish in.

And swimming up and down a
rectangle isn't very exciting.

Bambang started swimming faster
and faster. He raced from one end
of the pool to the other at a very
not **MEDIUM** speed. He made a

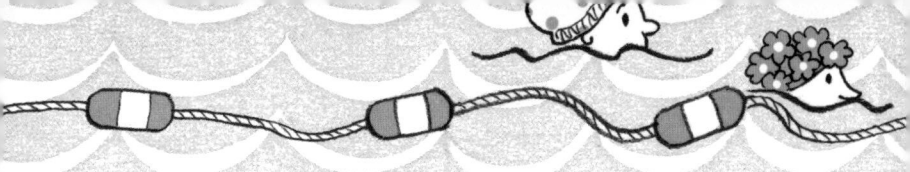

wave behind him which spread out
to the other corners of the pool. The
old ladies found themselves bobbing
in increasingly choppy waters. The
flapping man spluttered as water
swept over his moustache.

Then Bambang went zigzagging
under the water using his snout
as a snorkel.

 He swam right
underneath the old ladies.
He waved his snout
cheerily at them as he surfaced
on the other side. They waved back. The
man in the vest blew his whistle again.

"Keep in lane, pig," he said.

But Bambang had had enough of
lanes. He got out of the pool and shook
himself dry. He looked again at the
diving pool and boards.

"Let's try that one now. Can we?
Can we *please*, Mango?"

"Are you sure you'll like it, Bambang?"
Mango was a little doubtful. "Of course
we can."

It was a very, very long climb  to the highest diving board. Bambang started to feel less sure about whether he'd like it as he went up each rung of the ladder. Mango led the way.

At the very
top she stood
poised and tall
on the end of
the board, then
stepped off,
her toes neatly
pointed. She
landed in the pool
with a small *plop*,
sending out rings
of perfectly even
ripples.

Bambang was left on his own.
He peered over the edge, nervously.
In the distance Mango smiled up at
him. The water seemed a worryingly
long way away. He decided the best
approach would be to shut his eyes
and just run at it.

Bambang launched himself off
at considerable speed.

For a moment he was airborne and
free – the world's first flying tapir – his
ears and snout blowing upwards. Then
he made the mistake of opening his eyes.
Terror gripped him. Bambang shrieked
and bundled into a tight, tight ball as he
hurtled towards the water.

Water went EVERYWHERE.

Well, almost everywhere; not much was left in the diving pool.

"**Pig, OUT!**" shouted the man in the now dripping-wet vest. He couldn't even blow his whistle. It was too full of diving pool.

Bambang got **OUT**. He was mortified. He didn't even look for Mango. He didn't hear her shout, "Oh, Bambang, I'm so sorry! I shouldn't have left you up there. Wait! Bambang – COME BACK!"

He just ran.

Tapirs can run fast. They learn to when they're very small or else they get eaten.

Mango, who had never had to worry about being eaten, and who had to grab towels and clothes and shoes and all the other things tapirs are lucky enough to do without, could not keep up with Bambang.

In fact Mango Allsorts, hurrying out of the swimming baths, found she had *lost* a tapir. And though she *was* good at all sorts of things, she found this was one thing she was not good at AT ALL.

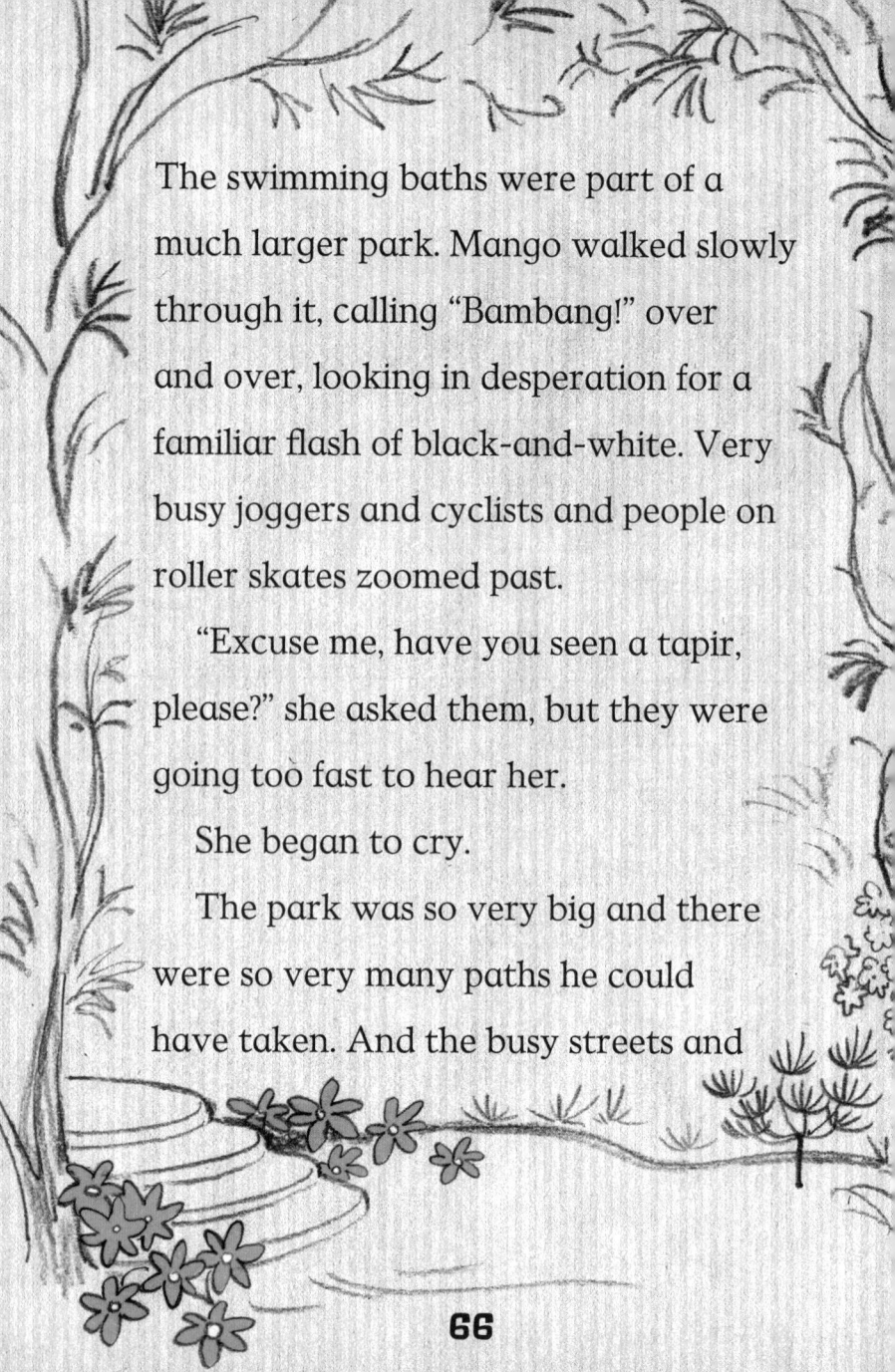

The swimming baths were part of a much larger park. Mango walked slowly through it, calling "Bambang!" over and over, looking in desperation for a familiar flash of black-and-white. Very busy joggers and cyclists and people on roller skates zoomed past.

"Excuse me, have you seen a tapir, please?" she asked them, but they were going too fast to hear her.

She began to cry.

The park was so very big and there were so very many paths he could have taken. And the busy streets and

tall buildings beyond the park were a befuddling maze. Mango knew that if Bambang had gone that far she would never find him.

She sat down on a bench. She felt hopeless. Her crying became the bigger, wetter, hiccupy, messy sort.

A large gold-wrapped toffee dropped from the sky into her lap. Mango stopped hiccuping and looked up, startled. A face was grinning down at her from the branches of a tree above.

"It's a good one. You look like you need it. Bad day?" the face said.

It was quite a grubby face, but friendly. It belonged to a boy.

Mango wiped her nose and eyes. After all, feeling hopeless would not find Bambang. She unwrapped the toffee and popped it in her mouth.

"I didn't know you were there. I've lost my friend," she said.

"I'm often up here. Nobody knowing is sort of the point. Everything's better in a tree. Fewer people trying to clean you up with wet flannels and make you put on smart jackets to stand on balconies and wave at boring parades," said the boy with feeling. "Who's your friend? How did you lose them?"

"He's black-and-white and people think he looks like a pig, which is stupid of them. He got scared at the swimming baths," explained Mango. "He often gets scared."

The boy looked thoughtful. "He's not a *tapir*, is he? A tapir in a ... swimming hat?"

"Yes!" said Mango. "Oh, YES! Have you seen him? Please, have you seen him?"

"Want to take a look?" The boy stuck a slightly sticky hand out through the leaves and Mango grabbed it and quickly climbed up.

"I'm George. Welcome to my tree," said the boy when she reached his branch. It was a bit of a squash.

George seemed to have more than the
normal amount of knobbly elbow and
knee. Also, quite a lot of stuff was stored in
his tree. He shuffled along to make space.
"Is that your friend?"

Mango looked where George was
pointing. Up high she had a perfect view
over the top of flower-beds and bushes.
Her heart lifted. For there, not too far
away, was Bambang.

He was sliding down the tail of a
golden horse; part of a park monument
built to remember the first man who
had ever been busy in the very busy city.
It was a statue in the middle of a pool
full of ornamental fish and water lilies,

WHEEE!

surrounded by a ring of golden fountains.

"Bambang!" she said. "Oh, that IS my friend! Everything really IS better in a tree! Thank you, George. I must go to him." She started to get down.

"That's OK," said George. "Can I come, too? I don't know many tapirs. Does he like toffees?"

"I don't know if he's ever had one, but I'm SURE he'd like to try. Just don't mention tigers," said Mango. "Or blow a whistle," she added.

Bambang ducked under a water lily at the sound of Mango and George's footsteps. But he popped out again as soon as he saw who it was.

"Where have YOU been?" He blew water at Mango, happily. "Look! I've found a much better pool. It has fish to play with, it's squishy on the bottom and the water stays in the pool where it's supposed to be. It smells right." He didn't realize he'd been found. He'd completely forgotten about running away. He hadn't known he'd been lost in the first place.

If Mango had been a different sort of girl she might have reminded him. She might have got cross. She might have told Bambang off for the worry he'd caused her.

Luckily, Mango was not that sort of girl.

So instead she introduced George.

And George introduced toffees.

And *didn't* mention tigers or whistles.

And Bambang found he *did* like toffees.

And they talked about city trees and jungle trees. And about city pools and jungle pools. And those who had shoes and socks took them off and paddled with those who didn't.

And everyone felt very pleased with everyone else.

And Bambang didn't miss anything any more.

Bambang
Puts On a
Hat

With a new pool, a new friend and, above all, with Mango, Bambang was truly happy. Mango was happy, too. But she was also a little wary. She knew that although there were no tigers in the very busy city, there were other dangers to a tapir of increasing curiosity. And some dangers were closer to home than Mango quite liked to think. She made Bambang promise never to go out without her.

So while Mango was at school, Bambang stayed at home. He was allowed anywhere in the apartment except the study where Papa worked all day and sometimes all night on his books. That had a big DO NOT DISTURB sign up. Bambang was careful to be quiet near the door. But when Mango's papa was lost in his balancing he seemed to forget about everything else. Including tapirs in his apartment.

EVEN MORE BUSY – please do not disturb!

Bambang passed most of his time sleeping or stretching or looking out of the window, but he did other things, too.

Trying on hats, for example. After the success of the swimming hat, Mango and her papa had lent him a small collection. Bambang found all the hats made him feel a little bit different.

He had a Being-Silly Hat,

a Thoughtful Hat,

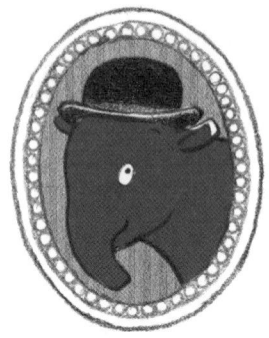

a Party Hat

and a Comforting Hat.

He also had a Very
Brave Hat. And one
particularly slow
waiting day, Bambang put it on.
It wasn't that he *forgot* his promise to
Mango, he just thought he'd take a tiny
peek out of the front door. As long as
he stayed in the apartment building he
wasn't really going out ...
was he?

Two of Bambang's favourite
wonders-that-weren't-in-the-jungle
were the stairs and the lift in the
apartment building. When he and
Mango went out together, he'd race
down all the stairs as quickly as he could
and see if he could beat Mango in the lift.
Mango always made sure he won.

Coming back up again, they would take the lift together. Bambang would stretch and press the top button with his snout. He enjoyed the strange jump in his tummy as they were *whooshed* up to the top floor.

But he had never been there on his own before.

The building was very quiet during the daytime. Everyone was out being busy. Bambang was pleased to have the place to himself. He was *not* very quiet.

Not *everyone* was out.

In the apartment on the floor below Mango's, Dr Cynthia Prickle-Posset had just returned from a long trip overseas.

If Mango, currently pouring one test tube into another at school, had known this she would have worried.

If she'd known about Bambang putting on his Very Brave Hat, too, she would have worried even more.

For Mango knew Cynthia Prickle-Posset was not a tiger. She was *much* worse than that.

Bambang galloped down the stairs and took the lift back up to Mango's floor three times. Then he decided to experiment.

First he tried bumping down some of the stairs.

BA-DOOM!

BA-DOOM!

BA-DOOM!

went Bambang's bottom. It was fun, but not very comfortable.

Next he tried sliding down them
back-feet first.

SHHLOMF-A!

SHHLOMF-A!

SHHLOMF-A!

went Bambang's tummy. It was interesting,
but a bit shaky-uppy.

Finally he climbed onto the banister and went hurtling down snout-first at top speed.

AIEEEAIEEAIEEEE!

went Bambang.

He landed in a heap at the bottom.

That, Bambang decided, was rather *too* exciting.

Upstairs, Cynthia Prickle-Posset had been listening intently. She started to unpack her travelling trunk. There was equipment in there that she would need.

Feeling slightly out of puff, Bambang began a slower exploration of the other floors in the building. As he got in the lift this time, he pressed each button in turn and had a careful look as the doors opened on each level. There wasn't that much to see. Most had bare walls and a front door, much like Mango's.

One had a poster up advertising dance classes. Bambang was impressed. He looked at what the couple were doing with their feet and had a go at

copying them. He was *not* successful.
He decided he would ask Mango about
taking the classes.

The next floor had a smart table
outside the door, with an enormous
vase of flowers on it. Bambang had
a drink of water from the vase.
All the going down stairs and
dancing had made him quite
thirsty. He made a *small*
mess. He hoped nobody
would mind.

This time, as he got back into the lift, a strange thing happened. The doors closed and the lift began rising without him pressing any buttons at all. Bambang felt nervous. A little of his bravery slipped away. He shut his eyes and hoped the lift was just taking him home.

But the lift stopped one floor short of home. When Bambang opened his eyes he saw the lobby of Cynthia Prickle-Posset's apartment. He saw Cynthia Prickle-Posset herself waiting for him, her finger on the lift's call button. And he knew straight away that he'd picked the wrong day to try on hats.

Home at last, Mango opened the front door of her apartment. "Bambang," she called, "I made peach flapjacks for us at school. Would you like some?"

There was no reply. No warm tapir rushed into her arms. No tapir tongue began licking her face all over. The apartment was silent.

Mango took a flapjack in to Papa. His books were having a particularly lopsided day. He had no idea that Bambang had gone.

Then, through the floor, they both heard a series of muffled thumps, bangs, shouts and awful shrieks coming from the apartment below. Now Mango was worried; dreadfully worried. She smoothed her hair and her skirt down, picked up her plate of flapjacks and prepared to pay a call on her neighbour.

Do you collect anything? Fruit stickers or especially smooth pebbles or pictures of cats, perhaps? Cynthia Prickle-Posset was a collector. She called herself a Collector of the Unusual. She travelled all round the world looking for Unusual Things. Her collection filled her apartment and spilled out into her lobby.

MOUSTACHES OF FAMOUS MURDERERS

Mango and her flapjacks had to squeeze through a jumble of the Unusual to find Cynthia Prickle-Posset's front door. Among other things, Mango saw an enormous jar of pickled puffer fish, a crate of assorted large bones, part of a rhino and a mysterious box labelled MOUSTACHES OF FAMOUS MURDERERS. She rang the bell, trying not to look too closely.

Cynthia Prickle-Posset opened the door a crack. She often looked red in the face, but she was quite scarlet today. She seemed a little out of breath, too.

"Good afternoon, Dr Prickle-Posset.
I see you've returned from your latest
trip. I do hope it was a successful one.
I thought you might like some flapjacks?
I made them myself." Mango was *always*
polite.

"Go away, Little Girl. I am busy and I
don't LIKE cake." Cynthia Prickle-Posset
was less polite. There were squeals
and banging and crashing noises
behind her.

CRASH! EEK! SQUEAL!

Cynthia Prickle-Posset looked round and started to close the door. Mango stuck out her foot to stop her.

"Only I've lost my friend, Bambang, and I wondered if you might have seen him. He's a tapir. Visiting from Malaysia," Mango added helpfully.

Cynthia Prickle-Posset turned a shade redder still. "I have NO knowledge of Malaysian visitors. Or –" she coughed "–TAPIRS. Remove your foot and return to your DOLLIES or whatever Little Girls like you play with. I have things to DO with my COLLECTION."

The banging noises behind her got even louder. Cynthia Prickle-Posset began to push at the door. Mango stood her ground.

"It's quite a noisy Collection, isn't it? Almost like something is trying to escape. Almost like something DOESN'T WANT to be Collected." She spoke in a louder voice.

"MANGO! Is that you? Oh, help! Help me, PLEASE!" Bambang's voice came from inside.

"Remove your foot NOW, or I shall FEED it to my giant carnivorous plant," said Cynthia Prickle-Posset, sharply.

Mango couldn't be polite any longer.

Bambang needed her. She
brought her other foot up in
a perfectly positioned
karate kick.

The door jolted
open allowing her to step past a caught-
off-guard Cynthia Prickle-Posset and
inside. Mango put down the plate of
flapjacks on a handy table made from
the shell of a giant tortoise and ran
to Bambang.

Poor Bambang. All of him was wrapped in an enormous net, and only half of him was squeezed into a glass case as well. Cynthia Prickle-Posset had obviously not been fully prepared for the sudden capture and display of a tapir. The case had contained a stuffed warthog which had been thrown on the floor to make room for Bambang.

Tapirs are rather bigger than warthogs. And live tapirs, not in the mood to be Collected, are even more difficult to fit in cases. Mango felt quite

proud of Bambang. Once upon a time,
he would have just curled into a ball.
Now, it was clear, he could really make
quite a big mess.

"Oh, Mango, I put on a Very-TOO-Brave Hat and went sliding and at first it was fun and then it wasn't and then I went exploring and at first *that* was fun and then it wasn't and you told me not to and I shouldn't have and now I've been Collected and I don't like it AT ALL!" wailed Bambang.

"I should think not," said Mango. "Now we're going to un-Collect you and take you home." She pulled Bambang out of the case and started to unwrap the net.

"What do you think you are DOING? BARGING into private property! Hands off that EXHIBIT. It is NOT for touching. That's my UNUSUAL WILD BEAST. THAT TAPIR IS MINE." Cynthia Prickle-Posset was positively purple now. She was also brandishing a *particularly* bristly broom at Mango.

Mango wished she was wearing a Very Brave Hat of her own. She felt horribly wobbly inside. She also knew she mustn't show the wobbliness. It wasn't so different from a tricky game of chess.

"We will be very pleased to leave,
Dr Prickle-Posset, and plan to do so
as soon as this net is off. Bambang
is not available to be Collected, you
see." Mango gave a final tug and freed
Bambang. "He is not *yours*, he is not
mine, either. He is not ANYBODY'S. He
is a guest in our city. Wild beasts, after
all, do not wear hats. And exhibits do
not eat peach flapjacks... Leave some for
our neighbour, Bambang!"

Bambang looked up,
a little shame-facedly, from the now
rather emptier plate.

"I'm very sorry," he whispered. "I was
unusually hungry. But usual in all other
ways!" he added hastily, in case he was
about to be Collected again.

Mango took a deep breath and
walked straight past Cynthia Prickle-
Posset and out of the door, Bambang
trotting at her side.

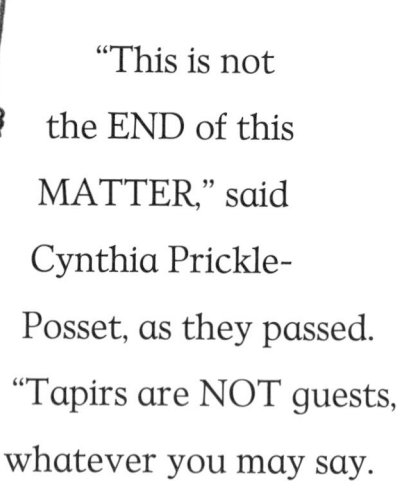

"This is not the END of this MATTER," said Cynthia Prickle-Posset, as they passed. "Tapirs are NOT guests, whatever you may say. They belong in ZOOS or in the hands of ADULT experts. You WILL be hearing from me again. I WILL HAVE THAT CREATURE."

But she stood down her broom.

Safe in the lift, for the time being at least, Mango and Bambang hugged each other very, very tightly.

"Oh, Mango," said Bambang finally,

"I promise I shall never EVER wear that hat again."

"Oh, Bambang," said Mango. "You shall wear whatever hat you choose. Always. But maybe not for the rest of this afternoon? Or at least not until after tea."

The Song
of the
Tapir

Bambang did a lot more curling into balls again in the days after meeting Cynthia Prickle-Posset. And despite Mango's gentle encouragement he did rather less trying on of hats, too. Mango, although still somewhat wobbly in her own tummy about the whole affair, said he wasn't to worry as their neighbour never stayed for long.

Mango was very relieved to be

proved right about this. A week later Bambang and Mango were returning with important supplies from the newsagent when they saw Cynthia Prickle-Posset leaving the building.

She was dressed in her full Collector's outfit and was loading lots of equipment into a taxi, which included a suit of armour, a lasso and a cage with iron bars. She was obviously planning to hunt out some *particularly* Unusual Things. Bambang shuddered. He hoped they would take a very long time to find.

Mango and Bambang hid, not terribly successfully, behind a lamppost.

They could feel the eyes of Cynthia Prickle-Posset watching them. She gave a loud **harrumph**, like an angry elephant. But then they heard the boot of the taxi being shut and the engine driving away.

Mango opened some of their important supplies to celebrate.

Even with Cynthia Prickle-Posset gone, Bambang still felt troubled. Mango had given him so much. He wished he could give her something in return.

And then he got his chance.

One day Mango's footsteps as she came home from school were slower and heavier than usual, a change only a finely tuned tapir's ear could hear. Bambang knew Mango needed a *particularly* loving head rub. She pulled his ears in a distracted way.

"Oh, phooey, Bambang. Phooey and pooh. It's the Big City Concert tomorrow and I just can't get my notes right. Papa's coming and I so want to be good. I've been practising and practising my clarinet, but the more I practise the worse I sound. I'm just NOT any good."

Bambang thought Mango was wonderful. He was her biggest fan. He KNEW her to be good at all sorts of things – making tapirs happy and safe, for instance. That was the best thing to be good at of all.

But he also knew that she was right about her clarinet playing. It *wasn't* good.

He stroked her face gently with his snout.

"Perhaps you don't have to play? Your papa will understand," he suggested.

Mango was stern. "Now, Bambang. We've talked about this before. If one gives up on things just because they're hard at first one never gets good at anything. Look at how good you've got at being brave about tigers and Collectors. That's because you've practised. I'll just have to practise all night." She looked determined. And a little sad.

Bambang nodded. Mango's attitude was inspiring. He just wasn't sure more practising was the answer this time. He had a think. Perhaps he *could* be of use?

"Sometimes," he said, gently, "music needs to be felt as well as played. What's the piece that you're playing tomorrow and what do you feel when you're playing it?"

"It's called 'City Nights' and I feel worried and cross," said Mango straight away.

"Then that's what we need to work on," said Bambang. His thought was clearer now. "And I know just how to help."

It was very nearly midnight. Mango was woken by a tapir blowing softly in her ear. She put on her slippers, picked up her clarinet case and followed Bambang out of the apartment. It was time for an adventure.

Have you ever been out somewhere you normally only go in the daytime very late at night? It feels quite, *quite* different and new. Standing in the darkness in her pyjamas, Mango bounced on her toes and clapped her hands.

"Oh, this is lovely! Where shall we go first?"

The streetlights made glowing pools. The dark shadows beyond their reach seemed extra black. But Bambang, even without a brave-making hat on, was not a bit scared of the dark. He knew his nose and ears would not let him down. He caught an interesting scent on the warm night-breeze and set off to follow it. Mango kept her hand on his shoulder. It was her turn to need a little reassuring.

They passed open doorways with the sounds of music and laughter spilling out. Mango looked in curiously, but Bambang didn't stop. The very busy city was less busy at night. People passing them in the street walked more slowly, arm in arm, chatting to each other in low voices. The vehicles were different and slower, too. Mango felt Bambang give a nervous shiver as the whirring brushes of a street-cleaning truck passed by. She gave him a squeeze. "No tigers. No Collectors, either," she said.

They reached the main square and here it WAS busy. A collection of small wooden stalls had been put up, all lit with colourful paper lanterns. They were selling many different delicious things to eat – the smells that had called to Bambang. Here, too, there was music. A group of musicians with stringed instruments were playing and people

were dancing. Mango bought a cone of nuts stirred in hot toffee, and a paper bag of fresh pineapple fritters. They shared them as they walked on.

"This is a wonderful treat, Bambang, but I still don't understand how it's going to help me play my clarinet tomorrow," said Mango.

"Just a little bit further."

Only when they reached a wide stone bridge did Bambang stop.

Running through the heart of the very busy city was a river. By day, its brown waters carried ships full of cargo and people in and out of the town. By night, it too was calmer. Mango and Bambang hung over the edge. They watched the reflection of the round, yellow moon swirl and shimmer in the current.

Further down the river, the end of the city and the beginning of the ocean were just in sight. Beyond that, a *long* way beyond that, lay Bambang's jungle. Everything was still and quiet.

"Now," said Bambang, "get out your clarinet."

"But I didn't bring my music with me," said Mango.

Bambang didn't answer. Instead he looked out to sea, lifted his head and began to sing.

All baby tapirs learn the Song of the Tapir before they can talk. It may be the oldest song of all, passed down unchanged from mother to child for hundreds and hundreds of years. Its simple whistled notes speak of jungles and tigers and love and loss and the niceness of bananas like nothing else can.

Very few people have ever been allowed to hear it. Now Mango was one of them.

She listened.

She felt.

She understood.

She picked up her clarinet and began to play.

Together, they made music.
They sent up their song; over the city,
down the river, out to the sea and the
beyond-the-sea. It was good.

The next day, in the concert hall, the audience was packed in. Bambang sat towards the back next to Mango's papa. He was finding it hard to remember he could be brave in a crowd and was trying not to curl into a ball. There had been some confusion on the door about the correct ticket price for a tapir. Nobody quite seemed to know, files had been checked and he'd heard the "**pig**" word muttered.

A lady with a bustling, almost Collector-ish air, dressed in an unfortunate dress of orange stripes, tried to squeeze past him to get to her seat. She made loud tutting and sighing noises.

Bambang felt panicky. Would it be better to leave now? There was still time to run. He started looking for the exit.

But he was stopped by the lights going down. There was a fanfare and the following announcement was made: "We are honoured to have the Governor of our great city and his family attending our concert tonight. Please show your appreciation for all they do."

Everybody clapped and a spotlight shone on a group of people in a box of extra-special velvet-and-gold seats, off to one side. Bambang, who couldn't clap, looked up and saw something so surprising that he forgot about finding the exit.

Standing next to the Governor, looking much less grubby but rather sulky was George-from-the-tree-in-the-park! Bambang waved his snout to say hello. George caught sight of him, stopped looking sulky and waved back. He lifted up a bag of toffees and winked.

The concert began. They sat through a rather loud trumpet, a rather quiet harp, a very screechy violin and a boy who played the mouth organ with his nose. Then it was Mango's turn. Bambang held his breath as she came out onstage. She looked smaller than usual on her own under the lights.

"I am going to play 'City Nights'."
Mango took a breath and lifted her
clarinet to her lips.

Then she let her breath out and put
her clarinet down.

"I *am* going to play 'City Nights'," she
said again. "But I'd much rather not play
it on my own. I have a very special friend
in the audience. Last night he showed me
what music can be. I play better when
he's with me. Bambang – won't you come
up?" Mango shielded her eyes from the
glare of the lights and looked out over
the rows of heads towards him.

Bambang froze. He didn't know what
to do. Could he get on a stage? Could he

face all those people? He'd never done anything like it before. But then he'd never done anything much except run and hide before he'd met Mango. How many of the world's wonders he had missed that way!

He could do anything with Mango. He would do anything for Mango. She'd asked because she needed him. Trembling but determined, he rose from his seat, walked down the aisle and up

on to the stage. He looked up at Mango
and she smiled down at him.

Bambang knew he was safe. He'd
found his home.

Mango put her clarinet to her lips
once more – and then took it out
AGAIN.

"In case anyone isn't perfectly clear,
Bambang is a tapir. Not a pig or a panda
or a badger or a horse or a skunk or a
rhino. A tapir. AND my best friend."

Then she put her clarinet to her lips and kept it there and they played together just as they had on the bridge.

And when they finished, the audience found their hankies and wiped their eyes and blew their noses and clapped and clapped and clapped, while Mango and Bambang bowed and bowed and bowed.

HURRAH!

BRAVO!

And every single one of that audience now knew what a tapir was.

Just like you do.